LIKE A THORN

LIKE A THORN

Clara Vidal

Translated from the French by Y. Maudet

DELACORTE PRESS

Published by Delacorte Press
an imprint of Random House Children's Books
a division of Random House, Inc.
New York

Originally published in France in 2002 by Éditions La Découverte et Syros
under the title *Mal à ma Mère*

Visit us on the Web! www.randomhouse.com/teens

Educators and librarians, for a variety of teaching tools, visit us at
www.randomhouse.com/teachers

Library of Congress Cataloging-in-Publication Data
Vidal, Clara.
[Mal à ma mère. English]
Like a thorn / Clara Vidal ; translated from the French by Y. Maudet. — 1st ed.
p. cm.
Summary: Throughout her childhood, Mélie believes her mother is two
people—Rosy Mother and Dark Mother—and she performs more and more
rituals to keep Dark Mother away as she reaches adolescence, when she begins
to realize that her mother is mentally ill and that Mélie may be, as well.
ISBN 978-0-385-73564-3 (hardcover)—ISBN 978-0-385-90552-7 (lib. bdg.)
[1. Mental illness—Fiction. 2. Mothers and daughters—Fiction.
3. Obsessive-compulsive disorder—Fiction. 4. Emotional problems—Fiction.
5. Family problems—Fiction.] I. Maudet, Y. II. Title.
PZ7.V6666Lik 2008
[Fic]—dc22
2007027997

The text of this book is set in 13-point Garamond.

Book design by Trish Parcell

Printed in the United States of America

10 9 8 7 6 5 4 3 2 1

First American Edition

LIKE A THORN

Mélie has two mothers. She's been certain of this since she was a little girl and saw a television cartoon about twin sisters. The twins were identical, but with totally different personalities. One was gentle and kind, the other bitter and cruel. Her mother is like that. Sometimes she's rosy and charming, sometimes dark and mean. So Mélie believes that her mother, like the twin sisters, must be two people, and the two share the task of Mélie's upbringing. Mélie doesn't wonder whether her father is aware of this or not. And she doesn't know which of the twins is her true mother. There are days when Mélie would like her real mother to be the gentle and kind one. Life is far more pleasant that way. But sometimes, when the dark and mean one cries a lot, Mélie pities her. She'd do anything to comfort the twin who claims to be unhappy and unwell. Would do anything to see her smile.

This is how Mélie's life unfolds with her two mothers, the rosy one and the dark one. Things are relatively easy: when her mother is in a good mood, it's Rosy Mom who's there; when she turns nasty, it's Dark Mom who takes over. The only thing to do then is wait for Rosy Mother to return.

This evening it's definitely Rosy Mom who appears at Mélie's bedroom door. Sweet and Rosy Mother. She's going to a fancy costume ball decked out in a long white and pink lace dress, with light flounces that puff down to the ground like clouds. Threads of gold dance between the flounces. Her bare shoulders are slightly covered with a transparent tulle wrap. On her head, a tiara gleams with shiny stones, adorned as well with a flow of pink and white ribbons. In her hand, she holds a sparkling magic wand, a gleaming star at the tip. There's no doubt about it: Mélie's mother is a fairy princess. With a tap of her magic wand, a doe or mermaid could easily appear in Mélie's room. Mélie wouldn't be the least bit surprised—because her mother is definitely a fairy princess.

Behind her mother's magical apparition,

Mélie's father grumbles in his ogre disguise. All this fancy dress-up bothers him. But he has to go. So he tries to make his impersonation more credible and growls, "I'm going to eat you, my child," sounding totally off-key. He's aware of it and says nothing more. Besides, Mélie has eyes for her mother only.

The dress, so light and ethereal, flows softly as Mélie's mother moves. Mélie would like to touch it, to feel the texture of the fabric. She'd like to kiss her mother's cheek. Her blushing skin looks velvety. Her mouth, red and shiny, reminds Mélie of a big cherry. But Mother anticipates Mélie's intentions and stops her.

"Don't come near me, the dress is very fragile!" she says.

Mother shakes her magic wand slightly and disappears, fading backward like a ghost.

Mélie is so dazzled by her mom that it takes her a long time to fall asleep.

As she sleeps, she dreams of a princess who gradually turns into a horrible and menacing witch, just like the ones in fairy tales. It is not a pleasant dream.

A picnic by the riverbank. A lot of people, a lot of kids. Rosy Mother is very joyful among her friends. She's the mom every child wants. She laughs and sings. She passes around a large bowl of fancy salad that she prepared. Compliments abound. In turn, others offer her a taste of their various dishes.

Mélie's father tries to look modest, downplaying his luck at having such an exceptional wife. Her moment of glory arrives at dessert time, when she shows off a basket filled with homemade baked goods. There are madeleines, meringues, and macaroons.

"You didn't make all that yourself, did you?"

"It must have taken you hours!"

"A pastry chef couldn't have done better!"

Mother goes from one to the other, holding out her basket, smiling, simpering. But the kids prefer the ice cream bars that someone else brought in a cooler. Mother is a little put out but doesn't let it deter her.

She abruptly grabs Mélie's hand and organizes a circle. All the kids join in.

"Ring around the rosie,
A pocket full of posies,"

sings Mother.

Mélie feels proud of her mom. All the

parents are looking at this attractive woman, admiring her way with children.

"Ashes, ashes . . ."

Round and round Mélie goes. Little by little she feels her mother's fingertips turn into talons.

It's no longer a hand that's holding hers. It's the sharp, pointed talons of a bird of prey that grasp her small hand like a vise. Mélie is scared. Dark Mother is here. She's taken the place of Rosy Mother without Mélie's noticing it. But it's Dark Mother for sure! Everything spins in Mélie's head. She'd like to free herself from the talons that grasp her hand, but they don't want to let go of her. Mélie keeps going around and around. She shuts her eyes. She no longer knows where she is. She catches her feet and tumbles in the grass. The other kids can't stop in time and fall on top of each other. They laugh, finding this very funny. It's part of the game. Mélie doesn't laugh. She's pale. Someone pours water on her face.

"It's the heat! It's too hot for her to dance under the blazing sun!"

Mother puts her arms around her. "Come on, darling. It's nothing. Really, it's nothing!"

She speaks loudly. She shakes her daughter. Mélie can feel the talons grip her shoulders.

"You're smothering her!" Dad says. "Let her breathe!"

He pulls Mélie away from her mom and lays Mélie down in the shade. Mother gives him a sharp look, as sharp as a sword edge. Mélie's chest relaxes. She sees her father above her. Dad is here, a half-smile on his face, full of words that he won't say.

"Are you feeling better?" is all he utters.

"Yes, I'm fine. Stay with me a little, Daddy, please!"

Mélie comes back from school with a fever, shivering. She has the flu.

Rosy Mother is there. When Mélie is sick, it's always Sweet Mother who's present. Thermometer, doctor, pills, syrup, nose drops. Sweet Mother is gentle and kind. She gives Mélie a new book and reads her a story. They are both lying in the small bed. Mélie cuddles in her mother's arms and listens as her mom reads another story, and then another.

Mélie would love to be sick all the time. She has no appetite but eats her vegetable soup and applesauce because Mother is here, close to her. She speaks to Mélie softly, calling her "my baby" and "my little darling." She whispers in Mélie's ear: "Pass your flu on to me. I'm grown-up and much stronger than you are. I can be sick instead of you." But Mélie wants to keep her illness. If she were sick all the time, maybe Rosy Mother would stay. Maybe . . . Mélie tries to prolong her illness. Three days. Four days. Five days. Her fever is gone but she says she's tired. She talks of headaches, of dizziness when she gets up, of nausea. From time to time, her father pays her a short visit. He doesn't know what to say to her so he comes bearing gifts, a doll's china set and a watercolor kit. All this lasts a long while.

So long that Rosy Mother has passed the wand on to Dark Mother.

"Well, you're not sick any longer, it's pure laziness," Mother says. "You'll have to get up now! I have other things to do."

Dark Mother is irritated, on edge. There are scary sparks in her eyes.

"I'm fed up with this mess, too! Look at this room! It's a pigsty! Now get up and tidy this place!"

Mélie hides the storybook at the bottom of a dresser drawer. It's Rosy Mother's book. When she returns, Mélie will take it out again. She tidies her room, feeling sad.

Mother is making crêpes in the kitchen. She holds a gold coin in her hand for good luck. She tosses each crêpe, giving the pan a sharp upward jerk. Mélie watches in fascination.

Mother laughs. She tells Mélie to give it a try. When the crêpe is cooked on one side, Mother hands the pan to Mélie.

"Your turn!" she says.

The pan is a little heavy. Mélie has to use both her hands. It's difficult to execute the flipping motion that seemed so easy when she was watching her mom. The crêpe takes off clumsily and falls astride the edge of the pan. She missed. Mélie looks at her mother furtively. She's relieved that her mom isn't angry. In fact, she seems amused.

"It takes a lot of practice, but you'll get the hang of it," Mother says.

Mélie feels reassured. It's definitely Rosy Mother who's by her side. The crêpes are delicious. There's one with sugar, one with chocolate, one with chestnut spread. The telephone rings. Mother leaves the room. She's gone a long time. And still longer. Mélie waits.

Mother comes back.

But it isn't her. Gloom and doom enter the room. Darkness surrounds Mélie's mom.

Her smiles have disappeared. Her jaw tight, she piles up the dishes in the sink and puts pots and pans away in the cabinets.

"Go off and play. That's it for now," she barks. "We'll finish later on!"

Mélie goes to her room. The crêpes feel heavy in her stomach. She's sorry she ate so many and lies down on the bed. She takes her teddy bear in her arms and holds him tight against her chest.

"I ate too many crêpes, Teddy Bear," she says. "I should have given you some. Why don't you take them from me and put them in your tummy? I have an ache."

Bristly spikes of black and violet seem to cover Mélie's mother. No one notices these spikes except for Mélie. She's used to them. When Dark Mother is around, the black spikes surround her. And when she speaks, even without shouting, her voice sounds like screams, giving Mélie the sense that toads and vipers are springing out of her mom's mouth. At least, that's what she imagines, because she's read it in fairy tales. But in reality, only ugly words and ugly sentences spout from her mother's lips.

"Bastard. . . . Scumbag. . . . I'll leave, that's what I'll do. I'll throw myself under a train. I'll blow my brains out."

Mother says many other things that Mélie doesn't understand. Today her father, grandfather, and grandmother are all in the living room. Gran is crying. Dad is shouting. His face is red. Grandpa is very quiet. Mélie makes herself small in a corner. No one pays her any attention. No one even knows she's there. She doesn't dare move. She can feel that she shouldn't be there. It's a grown-up discussion. And not a nice one. Not one for children.

After a while, her mother notices her.

"What are you doing here, Mélie?" Mother asks as she looks at her watch. "Oh, damn, I have to take you to the dentist. As if I need this right now! And we're already late! Come on, let's get going!"

Mélie feels shrunken as she follows her mom and climbs into the car. Mother starts off, gunning the engine as if to make it yell instead of her. She mutters to herself between tight lips. She clutches the steering wheel, her hands tense, shaking with anger. Suddenly she forgets that she's driving and starts zigzagging down the road.

"That bastard. I swear I'm going to run off!" she shouts.

Mélie is terrified. She starts to cry.

"Shut up, you little shit!" her mother shouts more loudly.

So Mélie cries even harder. She starts shouting as well. "Mom, stop the car! I want to get out! Stop!" Her fingers grasp the handle, ready to open the door.

Mother turns her head. "Mélie, let go of the door! It's over. I lost my temper, that's all. No need to fuss about it!"

Mélie keeps on crying, quietly. She wants her rosy mother. *Where* is her rosy mom? She doesn't want to be with this one anymore; this one is much too frightening.

At night in her bedroom, Mélie waits until everyone is in bed. As soon as the house is quiet, she turns on the bedside lamp and gets up. She begins by walking around the room ten times, saying, "Rosy Mother, Rosy Mother, Rosy Mother . . ." Then she walks around ten times in the other direction, repeating, "Dark Mother, Dark Mother, Dark Mother . . ." Ten times one way to call Rosy Mother back. Ten times the other way to ward off Dark Mother. When she's finished, she can finally go to sleep.

Mélie comes back from school. She hears voices on the terrace. Mother has invited some friends for tea. The weather is beautiful and they're seated in the rattan armchairs around the coffee table. There's gossip . . . gulps of tea . . . gossip . . . munching of cookies . . . Mélie knows all the guests. It's always the same group. The same women from the picnic, although only four of them. The best of the friends. When they get together, Mélie always has the feeling that her mother's voice becomes shriller. She uses a sharp tone that Mélie mentally refers to as the gossip voice.

"Mélie, darling, we're out here, on the terrace," her mother calls to her.

Mélie walks across the living room, her schoolbag under her arm, and kisses her mother, then the friends. They all have something in common: each one kisses absentmindedly, their lips as tightly sealed as unused buttonholes.

"She's growing so fast!"

"She's adorable!"

Mother adopts the proper attitude: she joins in the chorus of praise.

"Yes, Mélie is certainly becoming a young lady. And she's doing so well in school. Come, show us your notebooks, Mélie! She has lovely handwriting. And she draws beautifully. Get some of your drawings out of your bag!"

Mother places her hand on Mélie's elbow to encourage her to open her bag. Her grip is firm as she smiles and continues to sing Mélie's praises. Mélie's drawings trigger even more disproportionate compliments.

"She's an artist!"

"Not surprising, with such a mother!"

"She'll be famous for sure!"

Mélie feels uncomfortable. She hates these exhibitions, when her mother displays her like a circus dog.

But her mother doesn't stop at that. In a sudden surge of affection, she presses Mélie close to her and unleashes a flurry of endearing words.

"My little girl, my darling little daughter,

my love!" she gushes. Then she turns toward her audience. "You wouldn't believe how much we adore each other," she adds in a quavering voice. "Isn't it true, darling, that we adore each other?"

It's as if honey were dripping from her mouth. The friends are impressed by such abundant motherly love. Mother is triumphant. Maybe she expects applause, but Mélie recognizes her dark mother. She fell for her mom's charade at the beginning, but as soon as her mother took her in her arms, she felt the talons of the bird of prey she fears so much.

She has homework. She excuses herself to go to her room and get started. No one wants to keep the diligent student from her task. **Another** round of kisses into the void, and the gossip starts up again. Mélie tries to walk normally instead of running. When she gets to the hallway, she stares at the tiled floor.

One white tile, one black tile . . . She tries to walk on the white ones only, avoiding the black ones as if they were evil. She takes small steps because the tiles are small, making sure that her shoes don't overlap onto the dark ones. From that day on, Mélie will never put her foot down on the black tiles again.

For a while now, Mélie has had a stomach-ache. She complains about cramps that sometimes make her writhe with pain in bed. Her mother doesn't take her seriously because Mélie has no fever and isn't throwing up. However, one day, when Mélie refuses to go to school because the pain is too acute, her mother decides to call Dr. Brun, the family physician who has looked after Mélie since infancy. He's tied up but suggests that Mélie come by his office in the afternoon. He'll squeeze her in between two other appointments.

Attired in a somber suit, Dr. Brun is seated behind a shiny leather desktop. He pays no attention to Mélie; instead, he chats with her mom. Mélie wonders what she's doing here, folded over with cramps. The doorbell suddenly reminds Dr. Brun that he has other patients to see.

"So what's the matter with the young one?" he asks.

Mother answers for Mélie. "She's been complaining of tummy pains."

"How old is she?"

"Nine." Mother answers for her again.

"So no periods in the near future, I guess."

Mother lets out a short, sour laugh.

"Be serious, Doctor, she's still a little girl."

Mélie doesn't understand what they're talking about.

"We'll take a look. Take your clothes off, Mélie, and sit on the table, behind the screen."

Mélie removes her sweater, pants, and socks.

"Take off your underwear too."

"No."

"Yes. How else can I examine you?"

Mélie removes her underwear. Mother stands behind the doctor and watches.

"Lie down on the table here."

The doctor presses her stomach from top to bottom, from left to right.

"Fold up your knees. Open your legs a bit."

Mélie feels uneasy. She closes her eyes.

A finger penetrates her rectum. Mélie clenches her teeth. Pain. Fear. She wants to yell. What is the doctor doing? His finger moves inside her. With his other hand, he presses her stomach. No one says a word. Mélie opens her eyes and meets her mother's gaze above her head. Her mother is watching her with a cold, satisfied stare.

"So, Doctor?" Mother says. "What is it?"

Dr. Brun takes off his glove and throws it in the trash. "Nothing very serious. But it would be wise to have Mélie's appendix removed."

That night in bed, Mélie holds her teddy bear tight and cries without really knowing why.

* * *

No one in the family talks about anything other than Mélie's surgery. Everyone has been alerted. Mother organizes a dinner party with Grandpa and Gran and Mélie's godparents. The gathering looks like a Christmas celebration, with lots of gifts for Mélie. She opens her presents under the tender gazes of the grown-ups.

"Poor thing. They're going to do some unpleasant things to your tummy. But you'll see, it's nothing to worry about!"

"Nurses in hospitals are very kind."

"And you'll be there for only a few days."

"You know, an appendectomy is very common."

They make it sound like having a tooth pulled! Everyone has a reassuring little something to say, which makes Mélie worry all the more. The lovely blue-and-white-striped toiletry kit from her godmother makes her realize that she's going to leave home and sleep in a strange place, surrounded by people she's never met before. The musical toothbrush from her godfather, the pretty printed nightgown from Gran and Grandpa, all the gifts intensify the feelings of loneliness that well up inside her. It's as if she were going away for a long time. When Daddy hands her a new fluffy teddy bear, she bursts into tears.

"I want to bring *my* teddy bear along, the real one!" Mélie cries.

Her father is taken aback. "But you can pack them both. They'll keep each other company during your surgery."

Mélie likes the idea. She calms down. Then Mother hands her a large parcel that came from the bookstore.

"Here's something to keep you busy during your time at the hospital. I specifically avoided funny books because you're not supposed to laugh so soon after an operation. I know that only too well!"

Mélie's mom had taken advantage of their visit to Dr. Brun to reveal the circumstances of Mélie's birth to her. Her mother had undergone a complicated cesarean that nearly took her life. According to her, an appendectomy is a piece of cake compared to what she went through.

Mélie takes the gifts to her room and puts them in a drawer.

The day before entering the hospital, she packs old pajamas that are slightly too small but very soft, and the old book of fairy tales her mother gave her when she was ill with the flu. At the last minute, Mélie adds her old teddy bear at the very top, because she needs him to go to sleep. Her thoughts have been swirling with stories of open bellies: there's the one with the big bad wolf, in whose stomach Little Red Riding Hood and her grandmother were found; the one with her own mother enduring the pain and anguish of childbirth; and now Mélie's own stomach is about to be opened. What will they find in there? No one has told her. She only knows that something has to be removed.

Mélie is just coming out of the anesthesia and feels slightly nauseated. Her mother and father are seated on either side of the bed. Dad is silent but clears his throat softly from time to time, as if to signal his presence. Mother speaks in a low voice.

"All done, darling. It's over. Everything

went well. Are you in pain? Are you too hot? Are you thirsty? I'm sure they'll bring you something to drink."

Mélie doesn't know what to answer. Yes, she's vaguely in pain. Yes, she's vaguely thirsty.

"So, there you are, young lady," says a nurse as she walks in with a cup of tea. "All awake, are we?"

With Mother's help, the nurse lifts Mélie slightly and props her up with pillows.

"There, drink a little bit of this tea. It'll do you good."

Until now, Mélie has never tasted tea, which her mother says is for grown-ups only. Her mother drinks tea. Her mother's friends drink tea. Her grandmother drinks tea. But it's the first time Mélie has been offered any.

This will be Mélie's most vivid memory about her stay in the hospital.

Today Mélie is back home. Back to her room and her things. She reinstates herself in her familiar setting. But Mélie isn't quite the same as before. Mélie drinks tea like a grown-up now. Her stomach no longer hurts. All in all, she's glad she had the surgery. She was spoiled. She had lots of visitors. Mother behaved perfectly. Always there. Always attentive. Always sweet. Her father came every day too, always acting a little awkward but very caring. Some friends from school visited, and Brigitte, her best friend, stopped by twice. When Mélie left the hospital, she gave the nurse the pretty pink azalea that her mom had brought her.

It's snack time. Mélie is a little thin and needs to gain some weight. The doctor strongly recommends it. She finds her mother in the kitchen.

"There you are. I was just preparing some hot chocolate with slices of brioche."

"Oh, Mom, please, I'd rather have some tea," says Mélie. "I've gotten used to it," she adds with a knowing smile.

"Really! Well, you'd better forget the idea!"

Her mother's sharp reply sounds like a lashing. Mélie doesn't understand.

"But Mom, at the hospital—"

"The hospital is one thing." Her mother cuts her short. "You're home now. How stupid of them to give tea to a child! Now sit down and drink your hot chocolate."

Appendectomy. Hospital. Stomach. Tea. Grown-ups. All these thoughts swirl in Mélie's head. She doesn't want to drink hot chocolate.

"I feel funny. I'm going to lie down. I'll have my snack later on," she says.

Mélie goes back to her room. She's careful not to walk on the dark tiles in the hallway. She lies down on her bed and ponders things. While she was at the hospital, she thought a lot about this story of Rosy Mother and Dark Mother. She's old enough now to know that it can't be true, that it's not possible. But she's unable to abandon the idea because she doesn't know what to replace it with. And she needs to replace it with something—otherwise she feels scared.

At the hospital, she wondered whether she would walk around her room again once she got back home. She decided she wouldn't. If there was only one mother, it would serve no purpose. But it might ensure that her mother remained nice and pleasant all the time. Tonight, before going to bed, Mélie paces around her room again, but substitutes the letters *r* and *d* for *Rosy Mother* and *Dark Mother*. She walks round the room ten times one way, pronouncing the letter *r*, then ten times the other way, saying the letter *d*. This seems like a good compromise.

Mélie and her parents head to Italy on vacation. It's a long trip, and they decide to stop midway to spend the night at a hotel. There's one large bed, along with a smaller one, in the room. Mélie is supposed to be asleep. Her parents aren't. She can hear them talking in low voices so as not to wake her. She can't make out what they're saying but senses that the tone of the discussion is rising, growing more heated. It sounds like an argument, a controlled argument. She doesn't understand the words, yet it's as if they were echoing in the room like muted shouts. She feels a tingling on her skin, especially her face. She doesn't dare move, afraid her parents will guess that she's awake. The tingling turns into a burning sensation. Her head starts to buzz. Paralyzed, she waits for the approaching disaster and tries to figure out what to do to avoid the worst. She remembers that she learned about God in her catechism class.

Quickly, Mélie invents a prayer: "Jesus, please make them stop. Make them stop fighting. If the fighting stops, I promise . . . I promise you that every night when I walk around my room and pass in front of the crucifix, I'll say, 'Jesus, you died to save me, and I'm grateful to you.'"

It's a phrase she has learned by heart. She doesn't know what it means, but it's the only prayer that comes to mind. After all, you don't speak to God as you would to somebody else. You have to know special words.

The argument seems to have died down. The words don't echo as much. Mélie has an idea. Since she can't walk in circles here, she decides to count on her fingers, first one way, then the other, while saying the letter *r,* then the letter *d*. She does it ten times in a row.

The next morning, Mélie notices a red spot in her parents' bed. Her mother covers it quickly with the top sheet, but it's too late. Mélie has seen it. She knows nothing yet about women's periods and thinks that her mother has been hurt by her father during their argument. She looks at him, horrified. Her parents seem a little upset.

"It's nothing to worry about, Mélie," her mother ends up saying. "I'll explain later."

From that day on, Mélie will be scared of red. She'll never wear anything that color. She'll eat only overcooked meat. And she'll hate raspberries, strawberries, and cherries.

Mélie's mother feels unwell more and more often. She consults every doctor in town, one after the other, undergoing all sorts of tests and exams. The most renowned specialists get involved, looking into every possibility. No one understands what the problem is. Her illness has no name. She's a unique case. So she tries various treatments that are supposed to bring relief.

The top shelf of one of the kitchen cabinets is filled with her personal medications. There are pills of every possible color, shape, and size. Before every meal she pores over the prescriptions, scans the many bottles, opens one, then another, comparing them before deciding what to take, as if she had a choice.

At times Mélie catches a certain satisfaction in her mother's expression, almost as if her mom relishes the idea of swallowing one pill after another. She makes a big production of walking over to the sink, pills in hand, and filling her glass with water. She flaunts the medication so that everyone registers the extent of her suffering. Because that's what her illness is: a need to be noticed. Sometimes it takes the form of a backache, sometimes a stomachache, sometimes a headache. That's all anyone knows. There are no visible symptoms except for the discomfort that takes hold of her. All of a sudden, she'll look as if her legs are about to give way under her, and she'll hang on to a piece of furniture, her eyes half closed. She'll wobble for a bit, then collapse into the nearest chair, whispering, "I'm dying, I'm dying."

Her mom's behavior frightens Mélie, and she tries to keep her mother from falling.

"Mom, Mom, don't die," she pleads as she grabs hold of her mother by the arms. "I'm scared. Help!"

Most times, this snaps her mom back to her senses. She leans on Mélie's shoulder and drags herself to her room, where she lies on the bed.

"Leave me alone now," she moans. "I need to rest."

Filled with worry, Mélie concocts a magical formula to transfer her mother's discomfort onto herself: "Mom, pass your illness on to me. I'll give you my good health." She repeats the two sentences in her head until she's exhausted, so convinced is she that she's responsible for her mother's problems and condition. And convinced, too, that she can cure her.

One evening her mother serves dinner at the table, still feeling down after one of her spells.

"Did you tell your father what happened to me today?" she asks Mélie.

Mélie's father gives his daughter a resigned look and comes to her rescue. "Did you feel faint as usual?" he asks his wife.

"Well, not quite as usual. This time I really had the feeling that I was going to die. One of these days, it's going to happen. I'm sure of it."

"Stop talking like that! Can't you see that you're scaring the child?"

Mélie is busy drawing *r*'s on the table-cloth with her finger. Next to each *r* she adds an *h,* as in *health,* so that her mother will not only smile again like her rosy mother of the past, but so that she stays healthy, too.

Later, Mélie walks around her room, adding the letter *h* to her incantations.

Mélie is no taller or heavier than she was a year ago. One day she overhears her mother and Gran talking in the kitchen.

"It's not normal," says Gran. "There must be something wrong with her. Look at the Gautier girl, who's the same age; she's a head taller than Mélie."

"I know," Mother answers, exasperated. "She's such a trying child. She has everything anyone could want, and yet it's as if she's carrying the misery of the world on her shoulders. She's never happy, never hungry, and she never smiles. She's a pain in the neck! A real thorn in my side."

"Maybe you should take her to Dr. Brun," Gran says. "It could be a vitamin deficiency. She's reaching puberty, which might explain everything."

Mélie's throat tightens when she goes to the doctor. The memory of her last abdominal exam floods her mind. She doesn't want to repeat it. Fortunately her mother decides that her stomach is of no concern. She's focused on Mélie's pallor, thinness, and sadness. Dr. Brun looks at Mélie's tongue, listens to her chest, checks her reflexes. His diagnosis isn't alarming. Mélie again hears the word *puberty* without knowing exactly what it means. But neither the doctor nor her mother seems worried. Yet a sentence makes Mélie prick up her ears as they're about to leave: "A short stay by the seaside would do her a lot of good," says Dr. Brun. "Think about it."

The suggestion seems to please her mother. And the word *seaside* pleases Mélie. Could it mean a vacation? Mélie doesn't have to wait long to find out. As soon as her father comes home, she listens to her mother's version of the doctor's analysis.

"I saw Dr. Brun. Mélie isn't well. The only treatment he suggests is a stay by the ocean to restore her strength. I already contacted a place that was recommended down south. It's all settled. Mélie will spend the summer there. They can keep her for two months."

Mélie's mother rattles off all this information without taking a breath, as if it'll do her a world of good to be rid of her daughter. Mélie is appalled. Two whole months away from home! She casts a quick glance at her father, waiting for him to object and ask questions. He only answers a vague "All right, if it's for her own good." But Mélie can't believe that he's going to accept sending his only daughter God-knows-where for two months!

Mélie dares to look at her mother. "What kind of a place is it?" she plucks up the courage to ask. "I don't want to go. I'm fine. I'm going to eat, you'll see. And I'll put on weight. I don't want to go anywhere."

"The doctor prescribed it," her mother

answers curtly. "You're not healthy. Whose fault is that, huh?"

A feeling of shame washes over Mélie. Shame about being skinny. Shame about not growing. Shame about being in poor health.

"Two months will go by quickly," her father says, trying to console her.

Mélie starts to sob frantically. Her father doesn't know what to do. But his wife knows: she sends Mélie to her room to calm down.

"When you're sick, you have to take care of yourself," her mom calls after her. "Do you think we enjoy having a daughter in your condition? Well, we don't!"

Time seems to have stopped at the sleep-away camp. Mélie no longer knows how many days she's been there, or how many more days she has to remain. She's simply there, with no notion of time. She sleeps in a dormitory with about thirty other campers who range from eight to sixteen years old. She eats at a rectangular table for eight people, with a bench on each side. Every morning she goes to the beach for a swim. In the afternoon she takes a nap under a large canopy, on a folding cot. Then she goes for a walk in the pine forest. She participates in many activities. She's there while being absent, as if the reality of her situation is between parentheses. She speaks when necessary, laughs when everyone else laughs, even sings with the others without questioning why. There's a huge empty hole in her heart. She refuses to look into this hole for fear that she'll fall into it and die of loneliness. She's surprised to receive one or two letters each week, from her mother, from Gran, from her godmother. These people seem to belong to another life that she's no longer a part of. Yet she writes back, saying that everything is going well, that the counselors are great, that she has made a few good friends, and that she has put on three pounds.

Her letters make no mention of throwing up at night (nobody knows why), or of the day she almost chokes to death when she swallows a seashell. Neither do the letters mention her diving experiences, when she tries to stay underwater as long as possible to see how it feels to almost drown. The nurse advises her not to talk about it to her parents so as not to alarm them. Every day Mélie goes to the nurse's station to get treatment for the ugly pimples that have appeared on her legs and cause her pain whenever she goes into the ocean. But she's told that it's nothing very serious.

One afternoon after naptime, she's called to the visiting room. When she opens the door, her mother's loud laughter greets her.

"Hello, sweetie!" her mom says. "Surprise! We came to see you!"

Mélie has no time to react before being poked, examined, hugged, and covered with kisses and gifts. Her mother and father are thrilled and ecstatic about her healthy appearance.

"Look what we've brought you. Books, candy, a new bathing suit, a sun hat . . ."

Stunned, Mélie allows herself to be dragged outside, one hand for her mother, one hand for her father.

The day goes by in a whirl. Her parents came down south on the spur of the moment with some friends whom they left on a beach, giving themselves just enough time to see their darling daughter, whom they miss so much. They take Mélie to an ice cream parlor, then to buy a sundress and a seashell necklace. Soon it's time to go. They take her back to camp. She has to promise that she'll behave till the end of her stay. Mother hands some money to the camp director so that she can buy desserts for all her daughter's "charming campmates." A few more kisses and they are gone. Mélie never had time to say that she wanted to leave with them. That she didn't want to stay there any longer. That she felt abandoned and unhappy. That they had to take her back home. She lies in bed, rigid with sadness. She can't sleep. She wants to cry and throw up. Finally she does throw up. The nurse will say that her parents fed her too much candy.

The next day, at dessert time, the director announces that the peach pies are courtesy of Mélie's parents. Everyone cheers, saying how wonderful Mélie's parents are. They even decide to send her mom and dad a thank-you card signed by all of them. She's really lucky, Mélie is.

At the end of the two months, Mélie takes the train again, just as she did when she arrived, with some young girls who live in her area. They exchange addresses and promise to stay in touch.

During her time at camp, Mélie kept up with her evening rituals, but in her head only. She couldn't let anyone witness her strange behavior. They would have thought she was deranged. So each night before going to sleep, Mélie counted on her fingers while uttering her usual secret incantations, adding a few new words to reflect her present situation. She began and ended each phrase by saying "I'll be going home" three times.

In addition, during the day, she got into the habit of counting everything by sets of three. Three was the number that represented her family, her and her parents, when they were together. If she happened to walk on a leaf, she had to walk on two other identical leaves. If she touched a pebble, she had to find two others, and so on. It was complicated but crucial that she do this. She told herself that when she returned home, she wouldn't need to continue. She was wrong.

Mélie's life is more complex than ever. Her parents come upon her as she carries out her rituals, which are now numerous. "What's the matter with her? Did you see how she walks around and around? Why is she opening and closing the doors three times in a row? Why does she touch all the pictures along the hallway? Why is she constantly cleaning her glasses? What's going on, Mélie? Are you losing your mind, or what?"

Yes, Mélie is losing her mind. More and more so. Now Mélie thinks that her mother must be possessed by a demon who makes her sick and nasty. She decides to free her mother from that demon by using the power of her elaborate rituals. In addition to the magical incantations she intones when she touches things, or moves them around and puts them back in place, she spends long periods kneeling in front of her crucifix, begging God to make her mother well. She implores him to extract whatever carnivorous plant is gnawing at her mom's insides, its disgusting tentacles protruding from her eyes and mouth.

Mélie carries a pink kerchief with her, a symbol of the sweet, nice and rosy mother she believed in when she was younger. She stays away from the color black, which brings only sorrow and violence. Her phobia about red persists. She's in pain, in such pain all the time, but doesn't know where it hurts. There is nothing gentle in her life anymore, except for her brave plush teddy bear, who's been with her during all these tormented years. But the day comes when the teddy bear is no longer enough. Mélie yearns for a living creature she can call her own. She asks her mother for a cat. Her mother refuses.

"Don't you think life is complicated

enough? Do we need an animal to dirty everything, to scratch the armchairs and tear the curtains? Thanks a lot, but no!"

"I'll train him!" Mélie pleads.

"And what about my allergies? I'm sick enough as it is!"

Mélie abandons her desire for a cat and looks for another pet, one that won't damage the house. A hamster? Too dirty and noisy. Her mother would refuse. A bird? Same thing. A fish? Fish aren't the same. Physical contact isn't possible.

One afternoon, when Mélie comes back from school, she discovers a snail on the garden wall. It's pretty, with a brown and yellow spiral on its shell. Mélie pulls it away carefully and takes it back to her room like a treasure. A shoe box, a few pebbles, a bit of moss, a lettuce leaf . . . She puts a lot of love and tenderness into getting her roommate settled in. When the snail finally pulls its translucent body out of its shell and peeks out with its horns, Mélie is moved to tears. She picks up the animal gently between her fingers and puts it in the palm of her hand. The touch of this living creature on her skin, even if only over a small surface, brings her peace and relief. She starts talking to it in a whisper and feels instantly less lonely.

A few days later, her mother discovers her secret and the snail disappears. Mélie cries silently. But her sadness is familiar and almost sweet. After all, sadness permeates her everyday life, so escaping from the sadness would require a huge effort. It's much more comfortable to let herself plunge back into a cocoon spun with tears.

Mélie takes her teddy bear again and

cries into his ragged fur for comfort, almost at ease in the sour pleasure of suffering.

These days Mélie's main challenge is her walk to school. The rituals multiply along the way. Each irregularity in the sidewalk is subjected to an "obligation." The number three still rules. Each crack in the concrete, each parking meter, each sewer, dead leaf and piece of paper, everything that is on the ground has to be taken into account and multiplied by three. The feared conse-quence of whatever is red—traffic lights, car lights, clothing worn by passersby—has to be warded off by magical methods. Walking normally becomes extremely diffi-cult, and going from place to place takes far more time than it should.

In class, dictations have become Mélie's worst nightmares. She can't write fast enough, since her pen has to draw complicated arabesques before touching the paper. And she mentally assembles the letters of each word in sets of three, as well as the words of each sentence. Her mind feels as if it's working in overdrive, which disrupts her conscious work. She loses time, skips words, leaves blank spaces, so that it's impossible to grade her work.

Her French teacher summons her during a break to talk about it. Mélie pretends that she has difficulty hearing. It's easier to claim deafness than the illness she suffers from, and for which she has no name other than madness. This scares her too much.

After being informed of Mélie's problem, her parents make arrangements for audio tests, which prove satisfactory.

Everyone concludes that rather than having a hearing impediment, Mélie is simply not listening. She's moved to the first row in the classroom.

This brings no change. Just like the way Mélie walks to school, her handwriting reflects a chaos she can no longer hide.

Tonight Mélie's father is home. He's away more and more often, traveling for work. The atmosphere is charged. Her mother is in one of her bad moods, which have become all too frequent. Or so she pretends. She saw a new doctor today, who prescribed the same tests and exams she's gone through in the past, with no conclusive results.

Mélie's father grows irritated. He says it's all in her head. Mélie's mom answers that doctors are jerks and so is her husband. She says she knows what she feels.

Mélie busies herself at the dining table, organizing her table setting. She puts the plate between two red stripes on the white tablecloth, and the glass where two blue stripes cross. The knife and fork must not touch any colored part of the material. She meticulously moves every item until each is in its precise spot. After each mouthful, she takes care to put everything back in place with the same rectitude.

Her parents are still arguing but suddenly change the subject. Her father has noticed Mélie's behavior.

"Look at her!" he tells his wife. "Do you see what she's doing with her fork and knife? She's ill, just like her mother—nuts!"

Mélie stops suddenly, petrified, her eyes glued to her plate.

"What do you mean, nuts like her mother? You seem to forget that your family is the one with the moron. Maybe you're forgetting your cousin Roger!"

"Roger has nothing to do with this. He's not a blood cousin! And he's not crazy. He's a simpleton. This one, on the other hand, has a warped mind like yours!"

Mélie can feel her brain go blank. It's as if life were draining from her, together with a flow of urine between her legs.

Mother screams. "See what you've done, you creep! Call the doctor right now!"

Mélie opens her eyes.

She's lying on her bed. Mother is

pacing. She speaks loudly, full of agitation.

"Good Lord, what's the matter with her? What is it now? This child will be the end of me!"

Dad is at the foot of the bed. Silent. Upset. Uneasy.

Dr. Brun arrives. "So it's Mélie again," he says. "What's happened to her?"

Mélie feels as if she's bathing in cotton balls. She's present, but it's as if someone else were involved. Words reach her ears from a seemingly great distance: "Fatigue . . . nerves . . . fragile . . . adolescence . . . puberty . . . epilepsy. Epilepsy? No, not likely. Muscle twitching? Yes, could be. Rest . . . calm . . . vitamins. By the way, how was the camp by the seashore?"

"No, not the camp!" Mélie shouts.

"Why not, young lady?" asks the doctor.

"Your parents told me you gained four pounds."

Dad makes a huge effort. "I don't think the camp is the right solution for her," he says.

Mother looks daggers at him.

"Well, then. We'll start with vitamins," Dr. Brun says. "She's really not having an easy time with puberty. How old is she?"

"Thirteen . . . and nothing yet." Mother sighs. "*Nothing* is easy with her!"

Mélie's mother grows nastier and more peevish as Mélie's condition worsens. Mother accuses Mélie of making her sick. If she's crippled with pains, it's because of the worries Mélie gives her. One day she comes home triumphant, brandishing a large white plaster cast.

"Look what you've done!" she belts out to Mélie. "I'm having such back pain that I'm going to have to sleep in this contraption now, thanks to you."

At other times, she looks at Mélie, her eyes filled with rage. "When I think that I'm the one who gave birth to you!" she shouts. "What have I done to deserve this?"

She did give birth to Mélie, but what she doesn't know is that the very thought nauseates Mélie. To imagine that she came out of her mother's body is unbearable to her. Each time she thinks about it, she's disgusted and repulsed. One day the image of her birth becomes so vivid that she barely has time to run to the bathroom before throwing up.

Each night Mélie starts a new prayer: "Please, God, I beg you, let me not wake up tomorrow."

Each night before going to sleep, she repeats her plea, feeling increasing despair.

The girls in Mélie's class undress in the locker room and change into their gym outfits. Those who are beginning to develop show off their bras with pride—bras that have flower prints, polka dots, lace—each one nicer than the last. A bra is the ultimate item of feminine apparel, the symbol of womanhood that splits the class between those who have access to the adult world and those who are still little girls. Those who lie about having their periods can't do the same about their breasts. Mélie isn't menstruating, but she already has breasts. At home she stands tall in front of her mother, pushing her chest forward. But her mother avoids looking at her daughter's chest.

After completing a lot of incantations to improve her chances of getting a bra, Mélie decides to approach her mother.

"You know, Mom, I'm the only one in class who doesn't wear a bra. Even France wears a bra, and she doesn't need one."

Her mother looks Mélie up and down with snakelike eyes. "What did you say? Have you looked at yourself? What would you do with a bra, you poor girl?"

"But Mom, I have breasts!"

"Well, we'll see about a bra when you get your period. For the time being, you're still a little girl. At your age, I'd been a woman for a long time."

"But Mom, everyone makes fun of me in gym!"

"Really? Well, if you want to look ridiculous, then you can!"

The following day, Mélie's mother comes into her room. She's holding something.

"So you want a bra, to be like a woman," she says. "Look what I found for you: these were my breastfeeding bras. They're as old as you are, but I didn't have any milk, so they're brand-new. Feel free to wear them, since you have breasts!"

Mélie waits for her mother to leave and looks at the two bras thrown on the bed. She doesn't want to touch them. With a pencil, she lifts one by a strap for a closer look. The cups are each made of two pieces, held together with a satin ribbon, so that they can be opened for a baby to feed. Mélie doesn't know whether disgust, anger, or humiliation is her strongest feeling. She imagines herself changing in front of her classmates, wearing one of these bras.

"Bitch, bitch," she whispers between clenched teeth. "One day you'll pay for this." With her pencil, she carries both bras to the bathroom and drops them in the sink. "You can keep them," she shouts loudly enough for her mother to hear. "They don't fit me!"

She waits until her birthday and uses the money her grandmother gives her to buy the bra she needs. Now she won't be shamed in front of her classmates anymore.

On Mélie's birthday, another humiliation awaits her. Her mother outdoes herself. As she does every year, she invites Grandpa and Gran, along with Mélie's godparents. She prepares a good meal. Everyone seems in cheerful spirits. Cake time comes and Mélie blows out the fourteen candles. Lots of applause and wishes for Mélie's happiness.

The gifts are opened. Gran, always a good gift-giver, has bought the denim bag that Mélie badly wanted, and inside is an envelope containing the money Mélie will use for the bra. Her godmother gives her three nice T-shirts. As usual, her godfather has raided the local bookstore. Only a long, large box remains, which Mélie saves for last. It's her parents' gift. She doesn't dare hope . . . and yet the shape of the box . . . She unwraps it.

"Careful," her mother says. "It's fragile."

Yes, it's fragile. Mélie knows this. She

knows that this is the gift she mentioned over dinner one day, trying not to be obvious. As she removes the tape, she can feel her heart beating fast. A huge feeling of gratitude overwhelms her. How could she think so badly of her mother? What an ungrateful daughter she is! From now on, she'll behave perfectly, since her parents are so generous. The open box reveals a shiny black case.

With care, Mélie unlocks both hooks on the case and lifts the cover. A violin is lying on a velvet bed, a precious treasure. It's beautiful. Tears come to Mélie's eyes. She gets up and runs to kiss her mother, then her father.

"I wanted it so badly," she whispers in disbelief. "I'll learn fast. A girl in my class is taking lessons. I'll ask her the name of her teacher. Oh, I'm so happy, so happy!"

She takes the instrument out of the box, caresses it, puts it against her chin. She looks for the bow, wanting to elicit her first sound. There is no bow.

Mélie looks at her mother questioningly.

"You'll have to wait for the bow," her mother tells her. "You have the violin, now you have to deserve the bow. It all depends on your grades at school."

"I'm sure it'll motivate you to do well," Dad says with the usual awkward attitude he has toward his daughter.

Mélie is paralyzed. She doesn't speak. She puts the violin back in its case, her eyes downcast. She fears that the tears that are ready to flow from under her eyelids will gush out if she closes them. The last thing she wants is to cry in front of everyone on her birthday. No one speaks. The air feels heavy.

Mélie's godmother tries to break the stillness. "Until Mélie learns to play the violin, why don't we put on some music?" she suggests.

"Oh, not now," Dad says. "It's the start of the Grand Prix. Let's turn on the TV or we'll miss it."

With obvious relief, they all scoot in front of the television.

Mélie leaves the table and runs to her bedroom to cry. No one pays her any attention. She sobs on her bed, holding her teddy bear in her arms.

Mélie has one good friend, Brigitte. They've been friends forever. They live on the same street, two houses apart. Brigitte is the happy, cheerful type, always in a good mood. Happiness seems permanently affixed to her face, much like her prominent scar. As a toddler, Brigitte was bitten by a dog, and her left cheek bears a scar that resembles a patched hole. In spite of this, Brigitte is full of joy. Her parents adore her. They don't seem to notice the blemish on their daughter's cheek. Or they don't care about it. Mélie knows that they kiss Brigitte on both cheeks with no hesitation.

Since day care, Mélie and Brigitte have walked to school together, and they've grown up in the same class. At least, they used to go to school together. It's been different for a while. Brigitte is still happy and cheerful, but Mélie has become dull and somber. When Mélie started to change, her friend asked her why she looked so depressed. Mélie didn't answer. She doesn't want to talk about it. To anyone.

She herself doesn't understand what's happening to her. How could she explain it to someone else? Brigitte can only witness the change helplessly. She senses that her friend is drifting away, shutting herself within a world where no one can enter. Not even her closest friend.

Still, from time to time Mélie and Brigitte walk home from school together. They don't have much to say to each other anymore. They mostly walk side by side in silence.

"My mom is out this afternoon," Brigitte says today. "Maybe we could work together on our history project. I could come to your place."

No, no, I want to be alone, Mélie feels like shouting. But she's afraid her friend will ask why. They often did their homework together in the past, either at Mélie's or Brigitte's home. But that was before. . . .

"Sure, if you want," Mélie forces herself to say.

Mélie's mother is not home either. Now that Mélie is old enough to manage by herself, her mother has taken a job. Her work involves finding worthy objects for a friend of hers who is an antiques dealer. She spends days at auction houses, at flea markets, even at the homes of people who want to get rid of their old stuff. Now that she's working, she gives Mélie the most peculiar gifts. Her last present was a doll whose eyes were missing. She brandished it one evening above Mélie's bed.

"Look what I found for you!" she said. "Except for the eyes, don't you think she looks like you?"

Mélie screamed at the sight of the doll's frightening porcelain face. This made her mother laugh. Other presents include a doll's china set, each piece of it chipped. A deck of cards, each card torn or dented. A ripped fabric sewing kit, with only a broken needle and half of a pair of silver-plated scissors left. The gifts have become a nightmare for Mélie. She feels sullied by each of these damaged presents, and yet she's obliged to offer thanks as if they were precious objects.

The two friends sit atop cushions on the floor of Mélie's room, nibbling on cookies and a chocolate bar. Mélie is uncomfortable. She has the feeling that her room reveals traces of the rituals she performs each evening. She doesn't dare look up and busies herself by making two small piles of the cookies. Brigitte refuses to let silence settle between them and dives right into the heart of the matter.

"You know, Mélie, you seem strange

these days. I don't know what's going on, but you look as if you're having problems."

Mélie instantly lets go of the cookies. "No, I'm fine. Everything is fine. You're imagining things."

"I'm not so sure. You don't look the same. You never laugh. You keep to yourself at school. You seem as if you're always tired and in a glum mood. You just seem really down."

"No, I'm fine. I swear to you."

The conversation continues like this for a while, leading nowhere. Brigitte loses patience.

"Listen, you're my friend, or at least, you were my friend," she goes on. "Now I no longer know who the person in front of me is. You're like a zombie. So either tell me what's the matter with you or I'm leaving."

Brigitte waits a few seconds, then pretends to get up to go. Suddenly tears gush out of Mélie's eyes. Really gush out. The tears don't run down her cheeks. They positively pop out of her eyes and land on her knees, which she's hugging to her chest.

Brigitte moves next to her and puts a hand on her shoulder. "Come on, Mélie, tell me. You know I'm still your friend."

Mélie stays voiceless but keeps on sobbing.

Brigitte strokes her back to try to calm her down. Realizing that her friend won't talk unless prodded, Brigitte begins to ask questions.

"Is something wrong at school? I know your grades slipped, but they're still decent. You've always been a good student."

Mélie shakes her head, unable to answer.

"Is something wrong at home? Is it your

parents? Your mother? Are you worried about her? I ran into her the other day, and she looked really good. She was all made up and elegant, as always."

Mélie shakes her head, still crying.

"So it's your father? Or the two of them . . . together? Are they not getting along? Is that it?"

Brigitte stops talking. She waits for Mélie to finish crying. At last the sobs diminish. The tears are still flowing, but not as fast. Mélie's breathing is slowing down. She raises her watery eyes.

"Does your mother love you?" Mélie asks her friend.

Brigitte looks puzzled. "Of course she does. What a strange question. Your mother loves you, too."

"No, she doesn't. She doesn't even like me. In fact, she hates me. I don't know why. When I was little there were days when she loved me and days when she didn't. Now she hates me all the time."

"What makes you think that? It can't be true."

"No, I promise you, it is. She hates me. She hates me so much that it drives her crazy."

As she speaks, Mélie looks for proof of her mother's hatred. But her mom feeds her, buys her clothes, is affectionate toward her in front of people, so Mélie has a hard time finding any concrete evidence.

"Why do you say such things?" Brigitte asks. "Does she beat you? Come on, talk to me."

"It's not that. It's something else. She hates me, that's all. I can feel it. It's like claws that she plants in my skin. Like flashes of lightning coming out of her eyes.

Like toads coming out of her mouth when she speaks to me."

Brigitte is bewildered. "You're not making sense. You know, Mélie, you're not in a fairy tale, and your mother isn't a witch."

Mélie sighs. "The other day she gave me an old battered doll, along with a book that was missing pages. Another time, she brought me a broken candy dish with goop stuck to the bottom. And look, this is what she gave me for my birthday." Mélie digs out a supposedly antique bracelet and holds it up. "It's missing three pearls. Would *you* wear it?"

She brandishes the damaged jewelry under her friend's nose.

"*These* are my mother's gifts!" she shouts. "Just slaps in my face! They're all useless. She gives them to humiliate and belittle me. As if I'm not worth a real present. And you should see her sadistic look when I'm supposed to thank her. It's horrifying. That's *my* mother's love!"

Brigitte doesn't know what to say. She's now seriously wondering about Mélie's mental condition.

"I think you're—you're exaggerating," she stammers. "You probably have it all wrong. Mélie, what you're saying doesn't make sense."

"I know it sounds incredible. You think I've lost my mind, and maybe you're right. Sometimes I have the feeling I'm going crazy. I don't know where I stand anymore. I can't explain what's going on or what I feel. Yet the bracelet is real, you can see it. And if you look in the shopping bag at the bottom of my closet you'll find all my mother's other gifts. I'm not inventing them. Listen, Brigitte, you should go home now. I shouldn't have told you any of this. You just think I'm losing it. No one can understand."

Brigitte seems relieved. She hugs Mélie, telling her that she's going through a crisis and that it'll pass. And she leaves in a hurry.

After that day, Mélie feels lonelier than ever. Lonely in her mind. Lonely in her life. At school, she still exchanges a few words with classmates but keeps it to a bare minimum, talking only about homework, dates of exams, and teachers. But neither she nor Brigitte mentions their conversation. In fact, the two of them avoid being together.

Mélie isolates herself all the more in her distress.

Mélie is fourteen.

Mélie is fourteen and a half.

Soon she'll be fifteen.

Her ongoing ordeal becomes imperceptibly worse each day. Family members whisper that Mélie still hasn't gotten her period. Mélie's mother looks pinched and beleaguered when she answers questions from Gran, from Mélie's godmother, and from her friends who have daughters. No, Mélie isn't menstruating. When Mélie overhears this word in conversation, she feels like a lump of shapeless clay from which a young woman will one day emerge. For now, though, she isn't menstruating and so is unfinished. When you menstruate, blood has to flow out of you each month. And there's no flow from her.

At school, the girls who have their periods talk among themselves during gym or swim class. They do so with a kind of pride and mystery in their eyes. Mélie is the only one who doesn't participate in these conversations. Sometimes she affects a complicit air to make others think she's in the know. But she doesn't say much, afraid she'll say the wrong thing about a subject she's unfamiliar with.

Once, though, Brigitte asks Mélie if having her period makes her ill or gives her cramps. Mélie mutters that it doesn't—at least, not much. She's not sure if her friend believes her.

At long last, the big event happens. One morning after breakfast, Mélie realizes that her underwear is wet. She rushes to the bathroom, her heart beating fast. It's a shock to discover the first red stains on the white fabric. Strangely enough, this shade of red doesn't scare her. It's hers, made by her own body. She stays on the toilet for a while, contemplating the droplets of blood that fall into the water and dissipate like passing clouds.

Mélie is now officially a big girl, a woman. She conceals a pack of pads under her sweaters, at the bottom of a drawer. Hides the dirty ones in plastic bags that she throws away in public trash cans on her way to school.

Mélie doesn't mention the change to

anyone. Especially not her mother. She doesn't know why she hides this event that everybody has been waiting for. But that's the way it is. Over and over again she tells herself that she's a woman at last, just like the other girls at school. And also like her mother—precisely like her mother. Without Mélie's knowing why, this makes her sense danger. So she keeps the news to herself. She waits impatiently for the following month to see if the same thing occurs. Her period comes back. The next month as well.

It's been four months since Mélie's initial period, and Mélie's mother still doesn't know.

It's late in the afternoon.

Mélie is seated at her desk in her room,

working. Her mother comes in briskly, without knocking, as usual. She takes a look around the room, in case she spots something to complain about. Her eyes stop suddenly on the pack of pads that Mélie has left on the bed. She looks at her daughter, her face rigid and glacial.

"So it's happened! And you don't breathe a word to your own mother. How nice of you."

"I was going to tell you," says Mélie as she gets up to face her mother. "It just happened, I swear."

"And you'd already bought some pads, just in case?"

"I wanted to be ready."

Mélie has kept the secret for several months without knowing why. But at this instant, she knows the reason. She's ashamed. Ashamed to have become a woman, like her mother. Ashamed to be her mother's equal. It's as if she's appropriated a role she has no right to. She feels exposed. How could she, Mélie, so slight and sickly, dare join the ranks of womanhood when there's only one woman in the house entitled to that status? *Oh, Queen, you are the only Woman in this world,* whispers a voice in her mind. *But little Mélie has become a woman in her own right, younger and, who knows, perhaps more beautiful than you.*

Suddenly Mélie notices a look of panic, or worse still, of agony on her mother's face. Mélie feels dejected. She's waited so long for proof that she is blossoming into a woman, but it feels like the worst disgrace. She cannot be a woman—in fact, she does not want to be a woman—if it ultimately hurts her mother.

All she wants is to beg her mom for forgiveness. To ask for forgiveness and disappear. She wants to kneel in front of her mom and beg clemency for her impudence, effrontery, and audacity at wanting to be her equal. Just then she feels a flow between her thighs. She has been expecting her period, and blood soaks her underwear and trickles down her legs. Mélie doesn't dare move. She's frozen. In disbelief. Her mother watches. Stupefied. Horrified. Then a cry comes out of her throat, deep and strong, like the howling of a dying beast.

"Slut! Go wash yourself, you filthy pig! You're disgusting!"

Mélie gathers her short skirt around her legs as best she can and heads to the bathroom.

She stands in the bathtub, the water from the showerhead washing over her body. Cleansing her. She feels drained of everything. Of blood. Of tears. The water seems to dissolve her body, and, in a weird way, she feels taken back to a former state when she was only liquid. When she did not exist.

Mélie waits for death. To dissolve in the water and die. Her stomach is already dead. A stream of blood flows from within her like a wound that is still bleeding even though her body is no longer alive. The blood mixes with the water and flows toward the drain, where it disappears in a swirl, along with Mélie's womanhood. This lasts a long time. A very long time.

Now Mélie is no longer bleeding. No longer crying. The water has stopped. Mélie has gone from wet to dry. She's become desiccated.

Little by little Mélie sinks deeper and deeper into oblivion. She imposes an increasing number of rituals on herself, leaving her practically no time to rest. As soon as she wakes up, the chain of rites begins. There are things she must count, repeat, and touch. All the while she tries to protect her secret.

It's hell at home.

It's hell at school.

It's hell outside.

To hide all the time. To carry out actions so that no one notices, or notices as little as possible. She's terrified at the idea that others could see her the way she is, could guess what's going on in her head. That she could be caught in the act, confronted, and judged. "Mélie, you're crazy!" they would all say. "You should be locked up in a loony bin." Mélie would vanish. Would be buried alive between the walls of an asylum. Her mother rid of her at last.

Mélie grows frightened by this idea and becomes even more rigorous in the execution of her rituals. It's a stupefying paradox: as she tries to exorcise madness, she behaves like a mad person. As she tries to spare her mother, she irritates her all the more. As she tries to reassure herself, she multiplies her own anguish.

Mélie has no one to talk to. It's unthinkable to approach her mom. And her dad is rarely home. When he is, he kisses her in embarrassment, as if to say that he regrets not being able to help her. A coward, he dodges his daughter's distress and his wife's bitterness. Mélie's contact with her classmates is limited and superficial. But she has to talk to someone. It's crucial. Or she thinks she'll suffocate.

She decides to confide in Gran. Her mother's mother has always been kind to her. Mélie used to visit her often when she was little. She even stayed at Gran's over weekends and holidays and had her own room. Gran is the quintessential grandmother, plump and kind. Her welcoming arms and comfy bosom have soothed many of Mélie's sorrows. Lately, though, Mélie has kept her distance, just as she has from everyone else. But Gran is still Gran. Mélie knows that if she could speak to her, Gran would understand.

*   *   *

"What's going on, Mélie? You're so pale. Actually, you're always pale these days. And skinny, too. I don't like seeing you like this." Gran smiles. "Besides you're a real young lady now. You should be happy, laughing, and have lots of friends. Instead, you look so sad. What's the matter? Is it school?"

School. Always school! Mélie doesn't understand why adults pounce on school as the source of all problems. It's too easy to heap the blame on a bad grade or disagreement with a classmate.

"No, it's not school. It's home," Mélie says, almost in a whisper.

Gran retreats ever so slightly, as if her grandchild has uttered the wrong word. Home is obviously not the neutral territory that school is. It's more serious, more disturbing. Gran would clearly prefer to change the subject, before the catastrophe that she feels coming actually occurs. But Mélie doesn't give her the chance. In spite of all the difficulty she has speaking out, she persists.

"It's things at home that are bad," she says.

Gran tries again to minimize the problem. "At home? I see. Did you have an argument with your mother? You know, it happens a lot at your age."

"We're not arguing. It's a lot more than that. Yesterday I asked for a pet again and she brought me a dog she found in an attic."

"A dog? A real one?"

"No, a stuffed one. Or what's left of it. Two of its legs are missing and its belly is split open. All the stuffing's coming out. She was holding it by an ear, with the tips of her fingers, and gave it to me saying it would be quieter than a real dog. That all I had to do was sew up its stomach. When I mentioned the missing paws, she told me that my attitude toward handicapped creatures was improper. Then she burst out laughing."

Mélie says this in one breath, so that Gran can't cut her short.

"Oh, that's not very serious. It's nice of your mother to offer you a dog. It shows that she thinks of you."

"But no one would want that piece of trash. I put it in a bag at the bottom of my closet, with all the gifts she's given me. They're all the same."

"Your mom's in the antiques business, Mélie. She brings you back what she finds. It's kind of amusing."

"Gran, I've had my period for many months now."

"I know. Your mother told me. That's good. You're a big girl."

"When Mom learned about it, she said I was disgusting."

"Oh, come on, Mélie, I'm sure she didn't say any such thing."

"She even added that she didn't want to hear about it anymore. That I had to manage by myself and buy the pads with my own money, and that if I stained my underwear I had to wash it myself."

Mélie's grandmother feels uncomfortable. Under the pretext of putting something aside, she gets up from the couch where she and Mélie were seated side by side and goes to sit in an armchair, as far from her grandchild as possible. But Mélie is undeterred.

"Gran, Mom doesn't like me," she continues. "She despises me. I don't know why."

Gran's gaze becomes cold, like that of Mélie's mother sometimes. Her voice, too, turns icy. Mélie doesn't recognize her.

"You're imagining things. Your mother loves you very much," Gran says. "She's not a happy woman, you know. Your father— well, I'd rather not talk about it. But she deserves better."

Suddenly Gran's voice rises, filled with anger. "I really can't believe that you don't realize all she's done for you. You should be thankful. You should help her and be kind. She sacrificed a great deal for you. If you hadn't been born, I'm sure things would have been different."

Mélie doesn't listen anymore. It can't be true! Gran is siding with her mother. She refuses to see what's going on, or simply doesn't want to. Mélie's beloved Gran has joined the enemy. She doesn't like Mélie anymore. It's logical, after all. Mélie is asking her to choose between her grandchild and her own daughter. It's easier to doubt what Mélie is saying than face reality.

In a fog, Mélie listens to the justifications that are coming out of her grandmother's mouth like an unraveling ball of wool: Mélie is going through a difficult adolescence, like many young girls. She's confronting her mother, which is normal. Gran herself went through the same thing with Mélie's mom twenty-five years ago. That's how it is in every family: a conflict of generations. Nevertheless, Mélie is going overboard. She's ungrateful and selfish. And whatever the problem is, she can't talk about her mother this way. No one would have taken the liberty of judging her parents in Gran's time. All this is the result of today's permissiveness.

Gran offers Mélie some hot chocolate

and cookies to signal the end of the conversation. She doesn't realize that she was her granddaughter's last hope, and now the life raft Mélie had expected to hang on to for dear life is deflating.

Mélie pretends she has homework to do. She kisses her grandmother goodbye, taking care not to touch her cheeks with her lips. Then she leaves.

In the street, Mélie counts and avoids cracks as she always does when she tries to restore order in her mind, when she feels that she's falling. But like a volcano bubbling with lava, her thoughts are a series of eruptions. Mélie can't take it anymore. She wants to knock her head against the passing walls so that it explodes once and for all. But the people strolling in the street are looking at her. She keeps on walking, trying hard to empty her mind.

＊　　＊　　＊

Mélie staggers home as if she's been drinking.

"Where have you been? Do you know what time it is?"

Mélie doesn't answer. She goes to her room and falls on the bed. Her mother follows her.

"What is it now? What kind of scene is this?"

Mélie sits up and stares at her mother's snakelike eyes.

"Fuck you!" she shouts.

Agonizing. Immense. Irrevocable. Her mother is flabbergasted and backs out the door, her mouth agape. It's the first time Mélie has ever talked back to her mom.

* * *

Mélie falls on her knees in front of her crucifix. She starts to recite the prayers she knows: "Our Father, who art in heaven . . ." She bursts into sobs. "Good Lord, help me! You're abandoning me. I'm all alone. Why do I suffer so much? What did I do to deserve this? You gave me life only to hurt me. Who are you, God, to make people suffer this way? You already put your son on earth to have him die. What kind of god torments his own son and has him crucified? How could I love you? I keep calling on you for help, begging you, and you don't respond. I'm tired of seeing you on the cross, all year long, every Christmas, every Easter and All Saints' Day, tired of following your martyrdom all along the

Stations of the Cross. I'm fed up, fed up, fed up."

Violently, Mélie grabs the crucifix and throws it on the floor. The wooden cross breaks into pieces. Only the bronze body remains whole, and she squeezes it in her clenched fist until her hand hurts. She's bleeding on Christ's corpse. "Look how I'm crushing you. I'm killing you, since you came to earth just to be killed. But I didn't choose to be born to suffer, and yet I'm a martyr too. Only, no one gives a damn. I'm going to die unknown. No cross for me. No symbol of my death to exhibit to crowds. No one will be saved by my death. Dead for nothing. And where are you, you who came to save me, where are you? And how do you save me? As if I didn't pray enough!

"In the name of the Father, the Son, and the Holy Spirit," Mélie says as she crosses herself with the Christ figure, scratching her forehead, her chest. "And the mother? No mother. Only the Father and the Son. You're right. The mother doesn't count. She's just the necessary vessel that's discarded after use." Mélie hits her abdomen hard with the figure of Christ. "And the Holy Spirit? Who is this guy? Do I have to pray to him, too? Maybe that's my fault! I forgot to pray to the Holy Spirit. Forgive me, Holy Spirit."

All of a sudden, Mélie bursts out laughing, a crazy laugh, as she looks at what's left of her crucifix. "You see, I killed you too. You're dead again, but you're used to it. You get killed every day, every year, Good Friday after Good Friday, to make sure you save us. The more often you die, the more we're saved. In fact, I guess I'm saved, saved, saved."

She grabs a shopping bag from her closet and throws the fragments of the crucifix into it. "There you go, with the rest of my mother's gifts. Poor man. You thought you'd save us by giving your life for ours. Foolish me thought I'd save my mother if I suffered in her place. But I'm dying and she isn't any better. We're both in the same boat. We've both been taken for a ride, you by your father, me by my mother. And what are we left with? What are we left with, I ask you?"

Mélie falls asleep, exhausted.

Mélie's life has been shattered by her illness. Every spare moment is filled by one of her many useless rituals. Her grades at school have plummeted.

The school principal summons her mother. Mélie will never know what they say to each other, but by the scornful and triumphant look her mom gives her, she understands that they agree about the seriousness of Mélie's condition.

A few days later, her mother informs Mélie that she's made an appointment for her with a psychologist.

"Since you're behaving like a nut, you're going to see a specialist for crazy people."

Mélie is scared. A session with a psychologist seems like the first step to the asylum. It's the confinement she fears. The straitjacket. Horrifying images pop into her mind, similar to ones she's seen in movies and on television shows. Her life is over. Finished. Even if she were to be discharged from the psychiatric hospital, she'd never be able to obliterate the label INSANE that will be glued to her back, chest, and forehead.

Besides, Mélie knows she isn't crazy. If she were, she wouldn't know it. She wouldn't be aware of it. Sometimes she wishes she *were* crazy. She'd let herself glide into a parallel world where she wouldn't suffer anymore. But she's all too conscious of her suffering. She can see herself acting crazy. She watches herself powerlessly. It's as if someone else inhabits her body—someone she cannot control. Someone who has destabilized her mind and whom she can't chase away. It's as if she were possessed, but *possessed* sounds as scary as the term *crazy*. Both imply that she no longer has control of herself. Whether she's prey to a demon or deranged, the result is the same. There's something bad in her that's torturing and gnawing at her, and she doesn't know what it is or how to get rid of it.

* * *

Mélie's mother is out tonight. As usual, her father isn't home.

Mélie is in her room, puttering around, busily selecting, arranging, counting her belongings. She walks one way, then the other way. She thinks she's made a mistake. Does it again. Counts again. Checks once, twice. Her old teddy bear, dirty and bald, lies on her bed. She grabs it, holds it tight against her chest. She talks to it fast, to avoid thinking. Sings a song to it. Cradles it in her arms like a baby, just as Rosy Mother used to do with her when Mélie was little and sick. Mélie whispers the same words to it: "My little one," "My sweet love," "My sweetie pie." The rocking gradually turns into a slow clockwork rhythm, and Mélie hums a tune on two notes: "Sweet teddy, sweet teddy, sweet teddy." She abandons herself to the rhythm, swaying like a pendulum, oscillating from left to right, from right to left, left to right. She feels slightly dizzy. The words ring in her head: "Sweet teddy, sweet teddy, sweet teddy . . ."

In her trancelike state, Mélie stops thinking. She's somewhere else, in a world where nothing but the rocking and the words coming out of her mouth exists. Unaware of it, Mélie begins to nibble on her teddy bear's ears. Then the nose. Then the arms. She stops humming and gives out a throaty sound, a sort of death rattle, a grunt. Her nibbling becomes aggressive. She resembles a tiger, tearing its prey to pieces. Now Mélie can't contain the rage and violence surging within her. She starts pulling on the plush animal with her teeth. Pulls with all the strength of her jaws. Tears pieces of fabric away. The fur, all sticky now, has a dusty taste. She stuffs her mouth voraciously. But she doesn't swallow. She fills her cheeks compulsively. Stuffs in more and more pieces of plush, as much as her mouth can take. Her reflection in the small mirror in her bedroom is grotesque. Her face becomes monstrous, with two huge, outstretched cheeks. She keeps pulling on the plush and puts pieces into her nostrils. In one, then in the other.

Her breathing grows strained. She's suffocating. She panics. Wants to shout, to call for help. But no sound comes out of her packed mouth. She tries to eject some of the stuffing but risks breathing in some of the plush and choking. She thinks she's going to die.

In a desperate effort, she manages to pull out a chunk of the compacted stuffing, then another, and yet another. Some air reaches her lungs. Barely breathing, she has just enough energy to continue setting herself free from the snare. With care, she removes all the deadly stuffing from her mouth. She is exhausted. She's out of breath. Her mouth is dry.

The ripped teddy bear lies on the bed, among his torn, chewed, and spat-out bowels. He's dead. And Mélie is alive.

She doesn't understand why she acted this way. Why she wanted to die by killing her teddy bear. Why she chose to live. Why she decided to go on with her miserable life when she was on the verge of being liberated.

But Mélie is alive. She puts what's left of the teddy bear in the shopping bag, along with the crucifix and her mother's so-called gifts.

*   *   *

The following week, Mélie accompanies her mother to the psychologist.

As always, her mother dresses impeccably. She's wearing a light gray tailored suit, with a silk blouse and scarf. Perfect makeup. Hair well groomed. Mélie, on the other hand, is dressed in jeans and sneakers. Nothing to notice. Normal appearance. Just like any other girl her age. The waiting room is full of light, yellow like the sun. Soft music plays. Voices float into the corridor. A door closes noiselessly. The psychologist—a woman— steps in. She walks into the waiting room, looking as cheerful as the sunny room itself.

"Hello! I'll see you now, young lady," she says.

Both Mélie and her mother get up. The therapist intervenes.

"You're here for your daughter, madame, I believe?"

"Yes. But Doctor, I'd like to have a word with you before you see her."

"That won't be necessary." The therapist looks at Mélie, then back at her mom. "You don't have to wait for her, either. I'm sure she's able to get home on her own."

It's a slap in Mélie's mother's face. Her lips tighten.

"Oh, well, then I guess I'll leave."

She heads out, stiff and dignified.

The therapist looks at Mélie and smiles. "Let's go in," she says. "My name is Hélène. What's yours?"

Clara Vidal
lives in France.